Sticky Stuff

Written by Kate Walker
Illustrated by Craig Smith

An easy-to-read SOLO
for beginning readers

Scholastic Canada Ltd.
New York Toronto London Auckland Sydney
Mexico City New Delhi Hong Kong Buenos Aires

Scholastic Canada Ltd.
175 Hillmount Road, Markham, Ontario L6C 1Z7, Canada
Scholastic Inc.
555 Broadway, New York, NY 10012, USA
Scholastic Australia Pty Limited
PO Box 579, Gosford, NSW 2250, Australia
Scholastic New Zealand Limited
Private Bag 94407, Greenmount, Auckland, New Zealand
Scholastic Ltd.
Villiers House, Clarendon Avenue, Leamington Spa,
Warwickshire CV32 5PR, UK

First published by Omnibus Books, part of the
SCHOLASTIC GROUP, Sydney, Australia.

National Library of Canada Cataloguing in Publication
Walker, Kate
        Sticky stuff / Kate Walker ; illustrated by Craig Smith.
ISBN 0-439-97441-0
I. Smith, Craig II. Title.
PZ7.W15298St 2003   j823'.914   C2002-905284-X

5 4 3 2 1   Printed and bound in Canada   3 4 5 6 / 0

For my dog, Jasmyne, who is always stepping in chewing gum! – K.W.

For Kip, Emily and Doug – C.S.

For my dad, Jeremy, who is always
stepping in during a gunfight K.W.

For Edina, Shivaun and Doug C.B.

Chapter 1

Sophie set off happily for school one morning. She was winking at the sunbeams and smiling at the birds when, suddenly . . .

Splosh! Squash! She stepped in chewing gum.

It was the *worst* kind of chewing gum.

Horrible yellow chewy gum!

Thick as pudding! Globby as glue!

Eeeee! Sophie tried to pull one foot out.

EEEEE! She tried harder to pull the other foot out.
But it wouldn't come.

She was stuck to the sidewalk, like a lid on a paint can! Like an elephant in a vacuum cleaner! Stuck fast!

Chapter 2

Sophie's knees began to wobble.

Her stomach did flip-flops.

Most people caught in a mess like this would have yelled, *"Help!"* at the top of their lungs.

But not Sophie.

She looked at her feet.
Then she scratched her head.

Pretty soon she had an idea.

She reached down and untied
one shoe, and pulled that foot out.

She reached down and untied
the other shoe, and pulled the
other foot out.

And there she was!
Free as a bird!
Nothing to it!

Chapter 3

Sophie walked on, feeling very proud of herself. She smiled at the daisies and winked at the bees.

But then she saw that her brand new socks were getting very dirty.

Dirty as dust mops! Dirty as doormats! In fact, *dirtier!*

Sophie stopped.
She scratched her head.
Then she saw just the thing —
a park bench.

She hurried over, sat down, and pulled off her socks. Problem solved!

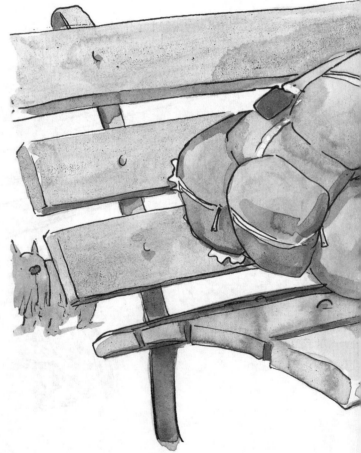

But when she tried to stand up . . .

She was stuck.
Something had grabbed her.
Eeeee! She struggled and twisted.
EEEEE! She wriggled and squirmed.

Her backpack was stuck to the bench with chewing gum!

With globby green bubble gum — a monster patch! Its big round monster mouth had latched on and wouldn't let go!

Chapter 4

Sophie gasped!
    Her eyes went wide!
    Her curls stood on end!

Most people caught by a globby green monster would have screamed at the top of their lungs, *"Help!!!"*

But not Sophie.

She clenched her teeth and scratched her head.

In less than a minute she had an idea. A really clever idea!

She slipped her arms from her backpack.

She took everything out — her lunch, her pencil case, her books. And then she said, "Goodbye, old friend."

It wasn't easy to walk away and leave her favourite backpack behind. But Sophie did it. She marched on, brave as a soldier, and only looked back once.

Chapter 5

Suddenly, in the distance, Sophie heard *Clang! Clang! Clang!* It was the school bell ringing.

She was terribly late.

Sophie ran to the corner.

She wriggled under the fence.

She sprinted toward her
classroom, and suddenly . . .

Zingggggggg!

Back she came, soaring through the air like a bungee jumper!

Like a plane doing loop the loops!

Like a fly zapped by a lizard's tongue!

25

Splat!

She landed back at the fence. Sophie was stuck *yet again* with chewing gum.

This time it was the *very worst* gum in the whole world. It was long, pink, stringy gum that looked like hundreds of spaghetti strands!

It had grabbed every one of her curls!

Eeeee! Sophie tried to pull free.
But —YEEOOOWWW! — that
really hurt!

She had to stop.
What could she do?

She was sure that if she waited
just a little while, a really clever
idea would *zing* into her head!

She gave her head a little
scratch to help the idea arrive.

Chapter 6

Just then, Sophie's teacher and her classmates spotted her through the classroom window.

They all came running. "Don't panic, Sophie!" they yelled. "We'll save you!"

They pushed and pulled!
And in no time *they* were all
stuck to the fence as well. Stuck
by their hair, their shirts, their
hairbands, their shoes!

They twisted and struggled!
They wriggled and squirmed!
But they only got stuck together
worse than ever. They ended up
like a lot of wriggling macaroni in
stringy pink cheese.

Like most people caught in a
terrible mess, they yelled, *"Help!!!"*
as loudly as they could.

Meanwhile, the really clever idea Sophie had been waiting for *arrived*.

She stopped scratching her head and reached for her pencil case.

She zipped it open and pulled out . . .

. . . a little pair of scissors.

With a few careful snips, Sophie gave herself a very nice, very brave, very modern haircut.

And there she was, free as a butterfly!

Free as the breeze!

Chapter 7

Sophie was about to set everyone else free when a police officer arrived. She brought her car to a screeching halt and jumped out.

Then a tow truck arrived.
Then an army convoy.

Then two fire engines . . .
an ambulance . . .
and a rescue helicopter.

Soon lots of people were working hard, trying to rescue the children and their teacher from the chewing gum.

They used ropes and ladders, saws and bolt cutters, cherry pickers and cranes.

And in ten minutes *they* were all stuck together as well! Stuck by their badges, their helmets, their gloves, their ponytails, their eyebrows, their beards!

All of them yelled at the top of their lungs, "HELP!!!" And Sophie knew exactly what to do.

Snip-snip! The teacher got a nice new haircut.

Snip! The tow truck driver got a shorter beard.

Snip! Snip! Snip! The children got interesting shapes cut out of their clothing.

The police officer lost her
badges.
A firefighter lost his suspenders.
The poor helicopter pilot lost
the seat of his pants.

But everyone was happy to
be free.

They raised Sophie on to their
shoulders and cheered.

From high in the air Sophie
could see over to the school gate.
And there were all the parents,
stuck in giant blobs of sticky stuff!

Sophie scratched her head.
She would have stayed to
rescue them . . .
    . . . but it was time to go home.

Kate Walker

I was putting away my best teacup when — *crack!* — I bumped it, and the handle snapped off. I hated to see it broken. It had to be fixed — at once!

It took only one small drop of superglue to stick the handle back on the cup. And stick my fingers together. And stick my shirt sleeve to the arm of the chair.

I stood up quickly, bumped the table, and everything — pens, books and telephone — fell off! Everything except my best teacup. It was stuck to the top of the table. I thought: There could be a story in this!

Craig Smith

Sophie in this story is very happy to be going off to school. She doesn't let anything stop her!

When I was a child I *didn't* much like going to school. I lived near an army camp, and I thought it was more fun to watch the soldiers. I saw them running with all their gear, and jumping out of helicopters. It looked so exciting that I wanted to join the army myself.

I enjoyed illustrating the part of the story where the army comes to help. It brought back lots of memories. But now I'm glad I'm an illustrator and not a soldier!